The Poetry Of John Oxenham

Volume 2 – "All's Well"

John Oxenham was the name used by William Arthur Dunkerley for his poetry. He used the named Julian Ross for his journalism. Dunkerley was born on November 12th 1852 in Manchester. He attended Old Trafford School and Victoria University, both in Manchester.

He married in America and lived they for a short time before returning to these shores, this time to Ealing in West London becoming both the Deacon and teacher at Ealing Congregational Church in the 1880's.

In 1913 he wrote a bestselling book of poems entitled 'Bees In Amber' followed by 'All's Well" in 1916. As a journalist he was a major contributor to Jerome K Jerome's Idler magazine.

In 1922 he moved to Worthing in Sussex and became the town's Mayor.

He died in Worthing on January 23rd, 1941.

Index Of Poems

FOREWORD

For those who were chiefly in my heart when these verses came to me from time to time, our men and boys at the Front, and those they leave behind them in grievous sorrow and anxiety at home, my little message is that, so far as they are concerned - "ALL'S WELL!"

Those who have so nobly responded to the Call, and those who, with quiet faces and breaking hearts, have so bravely bidden them "God speed!" with these, All is truly Well, for they are equally giving their best to what, in this case, we most of us devoutly believe to be the service of God and humanity.

War is red horror. But, better war than the utter crushing-out of liberty and civilisation under the heel of Prussian or any other militarism.

Germany has avowedly outmarched Christianity and left it in the rear, along with its outclassed guns and higher ideals of, say, 1870, its honour, its humanity, and all the other lumber, useless to an absolutely materialistic people whose only object is to win the world even at the price of its soul.

The world is witnessing with abhorrence the results, and, we may surely hope, learning therefrom The Final Lesson for its own future guidance.

The war-cloud still hangs over us as I write, but, grim as it is, there are not lacking gleams of its silver linings. If war brings out the very worst in human nature it offers opportunity also for the display of the very best. And, thank God, proofs of this are not wanting among us, and it is better to let one's thought range the light rather than the darkness.

What the future holds for us no man may safely say. Mighty changes without a doubt. May they all be for the better! But if that is to be it must be the work of every one amongst us. In this, as in everything else, each one of us helps or hinders, makes or mars.

If, in some of these verses, I have endeavoured to strike a note of warning, it is because the times, and the times that are coming, call for it. May it be heeded!

That the end of the present world-strife must and will mark also the end of the most monstrous tyranny and the most hideous conception of "Kultur" the world has ever seen, no man for one moment doubts.

But that is not an end but a beginning. Unless on the ashes of the past we build to nobler purpose, all our gallant dead will have been thrown away, all this gigantic effort, with all its inevitable horror and loss, will have been in vain.

It rests with each one among us to say that that shall not be, that the future shall repair the past, that out of this holocaust of death shall come new life.

It behoves every one of us, each in his and her own sphere, and each in his and her own way, to strive with heart and soul for that mighty end.

JOHN OXENHAM.

PART ONE: "ALL'S WELL!"

GOD IS
God is;
God sees;
God loves;
God knows.
And Right is Right;
And Right is Might.
In the full ripeness of His Time,
All these His vast prepotencies
Shall round their grace-work to the prime
Of full accomplishment,
And we shall see the plan sublime
Of His beneficent intent.
Live on in hope!
Press on in faith!
Love conquers all things,
Even Death.

WATCHMAN! WHAT OF THE NIGHT?
Watchman! What of the night?
No light we see,
Our souls are bruised and sickened with the sight
Of this foul crime against humanity.
The Ways are dark
"I SEE THE MORNING LIGHT!"

The Ways are dark;
Faith folds her wings; and Hope, in piteous plight,
Has dimmed her radiant lamp to feeblest spark.
Love bleeding lies----
"I SEE THE MORNING LIGHT!"

Love bleeding lies,
Struck down by this grim fury of despight,
Which once again her Master crucifies.
He dies again
"I SEE THE MORNING LIGHT!"

He dies again,
By evil slain! Who died for man's respite
By man's insensate rage again is slain.
O woful sight!
"I SEE THE MORNING LIGHT!

Beyond the war-clouds and the reddened ways,
I see the Promise of the Coming Days!
I see His Sun arise, new-charged with grace
Earth's tears to dry and all her woes efface!

Christ lives! Christ loves! Christ rules!
No more shall Might,
Though leagued with all the Forces of the Night,
Ride over Right. No more shall Wrong
The world's gross agonies prolong.
Who waits His Time shall surely see
The triumph of His Constancy;
When, without let, or bar, or stay,
The coming of His Perfect Day
Shall sweep the Powers of Night away;
And Faith, replumed for nobler flight,
And Hope, aglow with radiance bright,
And Love, in loveliness bedight,
SHALL GREET THE MORNING LIGHT!"

FOR THE MEN AT THE FRONT

Lord God of Hosts, whose mighty hand
Dominion holds on sea and land,
In Peace and War Thy Will we see
Shaping the larger liberty.
Nations may rise and nations fall,
Thy Changeless Purpose rules them all.

When Death flies swift on wave or field,
Be Thou a sure defence and shield!
Console and succour those who fall,
And help and hearten each and all!
O, hear a people's prayers for those
Who fearless face their country's foes!

For those who weak and broken lie,
In weariness and agony--
Great Healer, to their beds of pain
Come, touch, and make them whole again!
O, hear a people's prayers, and bless
Thy servants in their hour of stress!

For those to whom the call shall come
We pray Thy tender welcome home.
The toil, the bitterness, all past,
We trust them to Thy Love at last.
O, hear a people's prayers for all
Who, nobly striving, nobly fall!

To every stricken heart and home,
O, come! In tenderest pity, come!
To anxious souls who wait in fear,
Be Thou most wonderfully near!
And hear a people's prayers, for faith
To quicken life and conquer death!

For those who minister and heal,
And spend themselves, their skill, their zeal--
Renew their hearts with Christ-like faith,
And guard them from disease and death.
And in Thine own good time, Lord, send
Thy Peace on earth till Time shall end!

IN TIME OF NEED

Better than I,
Thou knowest, Lord,
All my necessity,
And with a word
Thou canst it all supply.
Help other is there none
Save Thee alone;
Without Thee I'm undone.
And so, to Thee I cry,
O, be Thou nigh!
For, better far than I,
Thou knowest, Lord,
All my necessity.

CHRIST'S ALL!
Our Boys Who Have Gone to the Front

("Be christs!" was one of W. T. Stead's favourite sayings. Not "Be like Christ!" but "Be christs!" And he used the word no doubt in its original meaning, anointed, ordained, chosen. As such we, whose boys have gone to the Front, think of them. For they have gone, most of them, from a simple, high sense of duty, and in many cases under direst feeling of personal repulsion against the whole ghastly business. They have sacrificed everything, knowing full well that many of them will never return to us.)

Ye are all christs in this your self-surrender,
True sons of God in seeking not your own.
Yours now the hardships,--yours shall be the splendour
Of the Great Triumph and THE KING'S "Well done!"

Yours these rough Calvaries of high endeavour,
Flame of the trench, and foam of wintry seas.
Nor Pain, nor Death, nor aught that is can sever
You from the Love that bears you on His knees.

Yes, you are christs, if less at times your seeming.
Christ walks the earth in many a simple guise.
We know you christs, when, in your souls' redeeming,
The Christ-light blazes in your steadfast eyes.

Here--or hereafter, you shall see it ended,

This mighty work to which your souls are set.
If from beyond--then, with the vision splendid,
You shall smile back and never know regret.

Or soon, or late, for each--the Life Immortal!
And not for us to choose the How or When.
Or late, or soon,--what matter?--since the Portal
Leads but to glories passing mortal ken.

O Lads! Dear Lads! Our christs of God's anointing!
Press on in hope! Your faith and courage prove!
Pass--by these High Ways of the Lord's appointing!
You cannot pass beyond our boundless love.

THE CROSS STILL STANDS!

"In the evening I went for a walk to a village lately shelled by German heavy guns. Their effect was awful ghastly. It was impossible to imagine the amount of damage done until one really saw it. The church was terrible too. The spire was sticking upside down in the ground a short distance from the door. The church itself was a mass of debris. Scarcely anything was left unhit. In the churchyard again the destruction was terrific--tombstones thrown all over the place. But the most noticeable thing of all was that the three Crucifixes, one inside and two outside, were untouched! How they can have avoided the shelling is quite beyond me. It was a wonderful sight though an awful one. There were holes in the churchyard about fifteen feet across." - From a letter from my boy at the Front.)

The churchyard stones all blasted into shreds,
The dead re-slain within their lowly beds,
THE CROSS STILL STANDS!

His holy ground all cratered and crevassed,
All flailed to fragments by the fiery blast,
THE CROSS STILL STANDS!

His church a blackened ruin, scarce one stone
Left on another, yet, untouched alone,
THE CROSS STILL STANDS!

His shrines o'erthrown, His altars desecrate,
His priests the victims of a pagan hate,
THE CROSS STILL STANDS!

'Mid all the horrors of the reddened ways,
The thund'rous nights, the dark and dreadful days,
THE CROSS STILL STANDS!

And, 'mid the chaos of the Deadlier Strife,
A Church at odds with its own self and life,
HIS CROSS STILL STANDS!

Faith folds her wings, and Hope at times grows dim;

The world goes wandering away from Him;
HIS CROSS STILL STANDS!

Love, with the lifted hands and thorn-crowned head,
Still conquers Death, though life itself be fled;
HIS CROSS STILL STANDS!

Yes,--Love triumphant stands, and stands for more,
In our great need, than e'er it stood before!
HIS CROSS STILL STANDS!

WHERE ARE YOU SLEEPING TO-NIGHT, MY LAD?
Where are you sleeping to-night, My Lad,
Above-ground--or below?
The last we heard you were up at the front,
Holding a trench and bearing the brunt;
But--that was a week ago.

Ay!--that was a week ago, Dear Lad,
And a week is a long, long time,
When a second's enough, in the thick of the strife,
To sever the thread of the bravest life,
And end it in its prime.

Oh, a week is long when so little's enough
To send a man below.
It may be that while we named your name
The bullet sped and the quick end came,
And the rest we shall never know.

But this we know, Dear Lad,--all's well
With the man who has done his best.
And whether he live, or whether he die,
He is sacred high in our memory;
And to God we can leave the rest.

So--wherever you're sleeping to-night, Dear Lad,
This one thing we do know,
When "Last Post" sounds, and He makes His rounds,
Not one of you all will be out of bounds,
Above ground or below.

BE QUIET!
Soul, dost thou fear
For to-day or to-morrow?
'Tis the part of a fool
To go seeking sorrow.
Of thine own doing
Thou canst not contrive them.

'Tis He that shall give them;
Thou may'st not outlive them.
So why cloud to-day
With fear of the sorrow,
That may or may not
Come to-morrow?

TO YOU WHO HAVE LOST
I know! I know!
The ceaseless ache, the emptiness, the woe,
The pang of loss,
The strength that sinks beneath so sore a cross.
"Heedless and careless, still the world wags on,
And leaves me broken ... Oh, my son! my son!"

Yet--think of this!--
Yea, rather think on this!--
He died as few men get the chance to die,
Fighting to save a world's morality.
He died the noblest death a man may die,
Fighting for God, and Right, and Liberty;
And such a death is Immortality.

"He died unnoticed in the muddy trench."
Nay,--God was with him, and he did not blench;
Filled him with holy fires that nought could quench,
And when He saw his work below was done,
He gently called to him,--"My son! My son!
I need thee for a greater work than this.
Thy faith, thy zeal, thy fine activities
Are worthy of My larger liberties;"--
--Then drew him with the hand of welcoming grace,
And, side by side, they climbed the heavenly ways.

LORD, SAVE THEIR SOULS ALIVE!
Lord, save their souls alive!
And--for the rest,
We leave it all to Thee;
Thou knowest best.

Whether they live or die,
Safely they'll rest,
Every true soul of them,
Thy Chosen Guest.

Whether they live or die,
They chose the best,
They sprang to Duty's call,
They stood the test.

If they come back to us
How grateful we!
If not,--we may not grieve;
They are with Thee.

No soul of them shall fail,
Whate'er the past.
Who dies for Thee and Thine
Wins Thee at last.

Who, through the fiery gates,
Enter Thy rest,
Greet them as conquerors,
Bravest and best!

Every white soul of them,
Ransomed and blest,--
Wear them as living gems,
Bear them as living flames,
High on Thy breast!

THE ALABASTER BOX

The spikenard was not wasted;
All down the tale of years,
The fragrance of that broken alabaster
Still clings to Mary's memory,
As clung its perfume sweet unto her Master.

Not less than Martha,
Mary served her Lord,
Although she but sat worshipping,
While Martha spread the board.

They also minister to Christ,
And render noblest duty,
Whose sweet hands touch life's common rounds
To Fragrance and to Beauty.

WHITE BROTHER

Midway between the flaming lines he lay,
A tumbled heap of blood, and sweat, and clay;
God's son!

And none could succour him. First this one tried,
Then that ... and then another ... and they died;
God's sons!

Those others saw his plight, and laughed and jeered,

And, at each helper's fall, laughed more, and cheered;
God's sons?

So, through the torture of an endless day,
In agonies that none could ease, he lay;
God's son!

Then, as he wrestled for each hard-won breath,
Bleeding his life out, craving only death;--
God's son!

Came One in white, athwart the fiery hail,
And in His hand, a shining cup--The Grail;
God's Son!

He knelt beside him on the reeking ground,
And with a touch soothed each hot-throbbing wound;
God's Son!

Gave him to drink, and in his failing ear
Whispered sweet words of comfort and good cheer;
God's Son!

The suffering one looked up into the face
Of Him whose death to sinners brought God's grace;
God's Son!

The tender brow with unhealed wounds was scarred,
The hand that held The Cup, the nails had marred;
God's Son!

"Brother, for thee I suffered greater woes;
As I forgave, do thou forgive thy foes,
God's son!"

"Yea, Lord, as Thou forgavest, I forgive;
And now, my soul unto Thyself receive,
God's Son!"

Thick-clustered in the battered trench, amazed,
They gazed at that strange sight ... and gazed ... and gazed;
God's sons!

The Christ of God, come down to succour one
Of their own number, their own mate
God's son!

And none who saw that sight will e'er forget
How once, upon the field of death, they met
God's Son.

A LITTLE TE DEUM FOR THESE TIMES

We thank Thee, Lord,
For mercies manifold in these dark days;--
For Heart of Grace that would not suffer wrong;
For all the stirrings in the dead dry bones;
For bold self-steeling to the times' dread needs;
For every sacrifice of self to Thee;
For ease and wealth and life so freely given;
For Thy deep sounding of the hearts of men;
For Thy great opening of the hearts of men;
For Thy close-knitting of the hearts of men;
For all who sprang to answer the great call;
For their high courage and self-sacrifice;
For their endurance under deadly stress;
For all the unknown heroes who have died
To keep the land inviolate and free;
For all who come back from the Gates of Death;
For all who pass to larger life with Thee,
And find in Thee the wider liberty;
For hope of Righteous and Enduring Peace;
For hope of cleaner earth and closer heaven;
With burdened hearts, but faith unquenchable,--
We thank Thee, Lord!

THY WILL BE DONE!

"Thy Will be done!"
Let all the worlds
Resound with that divinest prayer!
The joyous souls redeemed from ill
Know all the wonders of Thy Will;
Heaven's highest bliss is surely this,
"Thy Will be done! Thy Will be done!"

"Thy Will be done!"
Tis not Thy Will
That Sin or Sorrow rule the world.
Thy Will is Joy, and Hope, and Light;
Thy Will is All-Triumphant Right.
And so, exultantly, we cry,
"Thy Will be done! Thy Will be done!"

"Thy Will be done!"
It is Thy Will
That all Life's wrongs should be redressed;
That burdened souls their bonds should break;
That Earth of Heavenly Joys partake.
And so, right wistfully, we cry,
"Thy Will be done! Thy Will be done!"

"Thy Will be done!"
'Tis not Thy Will
That man should kiss a chastening rod;
But, heart abrim, and head to heaven,
Should praise his God for mercies given,
And ever cry right joyously,
"Thy Will be done! Thy Will be done!"

"Thy Will be done!"
It is Thy Will
That Life should seek its golden prime,
That strife 'twixt man and man should cease,
That all Thy sons should build Thy peace.
And so, full longingly, we cry,
"Thy Will be done! Thy Will be done!"

"Thy Will be done!"
Then Earth were Heaven,
If but Thy gracious Will prevailed;
If every will that worketh ill
Would bend to Thine, and Thine fulfil,
And with us pray,"Bring in Thy Day!
Thy Will be done! Thy Will be done!"

DIES IRAE - DIES PACIS

(As earnestly as any I crave the victory of Right over this madness of Insensate Might against which we are contending. As certainly as any I would, if that were conceivably possible, have adequate punishment meted out to those who have brought this horror upon the world. But I see, as all save the utterly earth-blinded must see that when the Day of Settlement comes, and we and our allies are in a position to impose terms, unless we go into the Council-Chamber with hearts set inflexibly on the Common Weal of the World, in a word, unless we invite Christ to a seat at the Board, the end may be even worse than the beginning; this which we have hoped and prayed night be the final war may prove but the beginning of strifes incredible.)

"Only through Me!" ... The clear, high call comes pealing,
Above the thunders of the battle-plain;
"Only through Me can Life's red wounds find healing;
Only through Me shall Earth have peace again.

Only through Me! ... Love's Might, all might transcending,
Alone can draw the poison-fangs of Hate.
Yours the beginning!Mine a nobler ending,
Peace upon Earth, and Man regenerate!

Only through Me can come the great awaking;
Wrong cannot right the wrongs that Wrong hath done;
Only through Me, all other gods forsaking,
Can ye attain the heights that must be won.

Only through Me shall Victory be sounded;

Only through Me can Right wield righteous sword;
Only through Me shall Peace be surely founded;
Only through Me! ... Then bid Me to the Board!"

Can we not rise to such great height of glory?
Shall this vast sorrow spend itself in vain?
Shall future ages tell the woful story,
"Christ by His own was crucified again"?

JUDGMENT DAY

The nations are in the proving;
Each day is Judgment Day;
And the peoples He finds wanting
Shall pass by the Shadowy Way.

THE HIGH THINGS

The Greatest Day that ever dawned,
It was a Winter's Morn.

The Finest Temple ever built
Was a Shed where a Babe was born.

The Sweetest Robes by woman wrought
Were the Swaths by the Baby worn.

And the Fairest Hair the world has seen,
Those Locks that were never shorn.

The Noblest Crown man ever wore,
It was the Plaited Thorn.

The Grandest Death man ever died,
It was the Death of Scorn.

The Sorest Grief by woman known
Was the Mother-Maid's forlorn.

The Deepest Sorrows e'er endured
Were by The Outcast borne.

The Truest Heart the world e'er broke
Was the Heart by man's sins torn.

THE EMPTY CHAIR

Wherever is an empty chair
Lord, be Thou there!
And fill it, like an answered prayer
With grace of fragrant thought, and rare

Sweet memories of him whose place
Thou takest for a little space!
With thought of that heroical
Great heart that sprang to Duty's call;
With thought of all the best in him,
That Time shall have no power to dim;
With thought of Duty nobly done,
And High Eternal Welfare won.

Think! Would you wish that he had stayed,
When all the rest The Call obeyed?
That thought of self had held in thrall
His soul, and shrunk it mean and small?

Nay, rather thank the Lord that he
Rose to such height of chivalry;
That, with the need, his loyal soul
Swung like a needle to its pole;
That, setting duty first, he went
At once, as to a sacrament.

So, Lord, we thank Thee for Thy Grace,
And pray Thee fill his vacant place!

ROAD-MATES
From deepest depth, O Lord, I cry to Thee.
"My Love runs quick to your necessity."

I am bereft; my soul is sick with loss.
"Dear one, I know. My heart broke on the Cross."

What most I loved is gone. I walk alone.
"My Love shall more than fill his place, my own."

The burden is too great for me to bear.
"Not when I'm here to take an equal share."

The road is long, and very wearisome.
"Just on in front I see the light of home."

The night is black; I fear to go astray.
"Hold My hand fast. I'll lead you all the way."

My eyes are dim, with weeping all the night.
"With one soft kiss I will restore your sight."

And Thou wilt do all this for me? for me?
"For this I came--to bear you company."

ALPHA--OMEGA

Curly head, and laughing eyes,
Mischief that all blame defies.

Cricket, footer, Eton-jacket,
Everlasting din and racket.

Tennis, boating, socks and ties,
Tragedies, and comedies.

Business, sobered, getting on,
One girl now, The Only One.

London Scottish, sporran, kilt,
Bonnet cocked at proper tilt.

Dies Irae! Off to France,
Lord, a safe deliverance!

Deadly work, foul gases, trenches;
Naught that radiant spirit quenches.

Letters dated "Somewhere France,"
Mud, and grub, and no romance.

Hearts at home all on the quiver,
Telegrams make backbones shiver.

Silence! Feverish enquiry;
Dies Irae! Dies Irae!

His the joy, and ours the pain,
But, ere long, we'll meet again.

Not too much we'll sorrow for
It's both "à Dieu!" and "au revoir!"

HAIL! AND FAREWELL!

They died that we might live,
Hail! And Farewell!
All honour give
To those who, nobly striving, nobly fell,
That we might live!

That we might live they died,
Hail! And Farewell!
Their courage tried,
By every mean device of treacherous hate,
Like Kings they died.

Eternal honour give,
Hail! And Farewell!
To those who died,
In that full splendour of heroic pride,
That we might live!

A SILENT TE DEUM

We thank Thee, Lord,
For all Thy Golden Silences,
For every Sabbath from the world's turmoil;
For every respite from the stress of life;
Silence of moorlands rolling to the skies,
Heath-purpled, bracken-clad, aflame with gorse;
Silence of grey tors crouching in the mist;
Silence of deep woods' mystic cloistered calm;
Silence of wide seas basking in the sun;
Silence of white peaks soaring to the blue;
Silence of dawnings, when, their matins sung,
The little birds do fall asleep again;
For the deep silence of high golden noons;
Silence of gloamings and the setting sun;
Silence of moonlit nights and patterned glades;
Silence of stars, magnificently still,
Yet ever chanting their Creator's skill;
For that high silence of Thine Open House,
Dim-branching roof and lofty-pillared aisle,
Where burdened hearts find rest in Thee awhile;
Silence of friendship, telling more than words;
Silence of hearts, close-knitting heart to heart
Silence of joys too wonderful for words;
Silence of sorrows, when Thou drawest near;
Silence of soul, wherein we come to Thee,
And find ourselves in Thine Immensity;
For that great silence where Thou dwell'st alone
Father, Spirit, Son, in One,
Keeping watch above Thine Own,
Deep unto deep, within us sound sweet chords
Of praise beyond the reach of human words;
In our souls' silence, feeling only Thee,
We thank Thee, thank Thee,
Thank Thee, Lord!

THE NAMELESS GRAVES

Unnamed at times, at times unknown,
Our graves lie thick beyond the seas;
Unnamed, but not of Him unknown;
He knows! He sees!

And not one soul has fallen in vain.

Here was no useless sacrifice.
From this red sowing of white seed
New life shall rise.

All that for which they fought lives on,
And flourishes triumphantly;
Watered with blood and hopeful tears,
It could not die.

The world was sinking in a slough
Of sloth, and ease, and selfish greed;
God surely sent this scourge to mould
A nobler creed.

Birth comes with travail; all these woes
Are birth-pangs of the days to be.
Life's noblest things are ever born
In agony.

So comfort to the stricken heart!
Take solace in the thought that he
You mourn was called by God to such
High dignity.

BLINDED!
You that still have your sight,
Remember me!
I risked my life, I lost my eyes,
That you might see.

Now in the dark I go,
That you have light.
Yours, all the joy of day,
I have but night.

Yours still, the faces dear,
The fields, the sky.
For me, ah me! there's nought
But this black misery!

In this unending night,
I can but see
What once I saw, and fain
Would see again.
O, midnight of black pain!
Come, Comrade Death,
Come quick, and set me free,
And give me back my eyes again!

Nay then, Christ's vicar,

You who bear our pain,
Ours be it now to see
Your dark days lighted,
And your way made plain.

SAID THE WOUNDED ONE
Just see that we get full value
Of that for which we have paid.
The price has been a heavy one,
But the goods are there and we've paid.
We've paid in our toil and our woundings;
We've paid in the blood we've shed;
We've paid in our bitter hardships;
We've paid with our many dead.

It's not payment in kind we ask for,
Two wrongs don't make much of a right.
All we ask is that, what we have paid for,
You secure for us, all right and tight.

The Peace of the World's what we're after;
We've all had enough of King Cain,
And the Kaiser and all his bully-men,
With their World-Power big on the brain.

No! we fought with a definite object,
And it's this and we want it made plain,
That it's God, and not any devil,
That's to rule in the world again,

OUR SHARE
And we ourselves? Are our hands clean?
Are our souls free from blame
For this world-tragedy?
Nay then! Like all the rest,
We had relaxed our hold on higher things,
And satisfied ourselves with smaller.
Ease, pleasure, greed of gold,
Laxed morals even in these,
We suffered them, as unaware
Of their soul-cankerings.
We had slipped back along the sloping way,
No longer holding First Things First,
But throning gods emasculate,
Idols of our own fashioning,
Heads of sham gold and feet of crumbling clay.
If we would build anew, and build to stay,
We must find God again,
And go His way.

POLICEMAN X
"Shall it be Peace?
A voice within me cried and would not cease,
'One man could do it if he would but dare.'"
(From "Policeman X" in "Bees in Amber.")

EPILOGUE, 1914
He did not dare!
His swelling pride laid wait
On opportunity, then dropped the mask
And tempted Fate, cast loaded dice, and lost;
Nor recked the cost of losing.

"Their souls are mine.
Their lives were in thy hand;
Of thee I do require them!"

The Voice, so stern and sad, thrilled my heart's core
And shook me where I stood.
Sharper than sharpest sword, it fell on him
Who stood defiant, muffle-cloaked and helmed,
With eyes that burned, impatient to be gone.

"The fetor of thy grim burnt offerings
Comes up to me in clouds of bitterness.
Thy fell undoings crucify afresh
Thy Lord who died alike for these and thee.
Thy works are Death; thy spear is in my side,
O man! O man! was it for this I died?

Was it for this?
A valiant people harried, to the void,
Their fruitful fields a burnt-out wilderness,
Their prosperous country ravelled into waste,
Their smiling land a vast red sepulchre.
Thy work!

For this?
Black clouds of smoke that vail the sight of heaven;
Black piles of stones which yesterday were homes;
And raw black heaps which once were villages;
Fair towns in ashes, spoiled to suage thy spleen;
My temples desecrate, My priests out-cast;
Black ruin everywhere, and red, a land
All swamped with blood, and savaged raw and bare;
All sickened with the reek and stench of war,
And flung a prey to pestilence and want;
Thy work!

For this?
Life's fair white flower of manhood in the dust;
Ten thousand thousand hearts made desolate;
My troubled world a seething pit of hate;
My helpless ones the victims of thy lust;
The broken maids lift hopeless eyes to Me,
The little ones lift handless arms to Me,
The tortured women lift white lips to Me,
The eyes of murdered white-haired sires and dames
Stare up at Me. And the sad anguished eyes
Of My dumb beasts in agony.
Thy work!

Outrage on outrage thunders to the sky
The tale of thy stupendous infamy,
Thy slaughterings, thy treacheries, thy thefts,
Thy broken pacts, thy honour in the mire,
Thy poor humanity cast off to sate thy pride;
'Twere better thou hadst never lived, or died
Ere come to this.
Thou art the man! The scales were in thy hand.
For this vast wrong I hold thy soul in fee.
Seek not a scapegoat for thy righteous due,
Nor hope to void thy countability.
Until thou purge thy pride and turn to Me,
As thou hast done, so be it unto thee!"

The shining eyes, so stern, and sweet, and sad,
Searched the hard face for sign of hopeful grace.
But grace was none. Enarmoured in his pride,
With brusque salute the other turned, and strode
Adown the night of Death and fitful fires.

Then, as the Master bowed him, sorrowing,
I heard a great Voice pealing through the heavens,
A Voice that dwarfed earth's thunders to a moan:
Woe! Woe! Woe! to him by whom this came.
His house shall unto him be desolate.
And, to the end of time, his name shall be
A byword and reproach in all the lands
He rapined ... And his own shall curse him
For the ruin that he brought.
Who without reason draws the sword
By sword shall perish!
The Lord hath said ... So be it, Lord!"

AND AFTER! ....
.... WHAT?

God grant the sacrifice be not in vain!

Those valiant souls who set themselves with pride
To hold the Ways ... and fought ... and fought ... and died,
They rest with Thee.
But, to the end of time,
The virtue of their valiance shall remain,
To pulse a nobler life through every vein
Of our humanity.

No drop of hero-blood e'er runs to waste,
But springs eternal, Fountain pure and chaste,
For cleansing of men's souls from earthly grime.
Life knows no waste. The Reaper tolls in vain,
In vain piles high his grim red harvesting,
His dread, red harvest of the slain!
God's wondrous husbandry is oft obscure,
But, without halt or haste, its course is sure,
And His good grain must die to live again.

From this dread sowing, grant us harvest, Lord,
Of Nobler Doing, and of Loftier Hope,
An All-Embracing and Enduring Peace,
A Bond of States, a Pact of Peoples, based
On no caprice of royal whim, but on
Foundation mightier than the mightiest throne
The Well-Considered Will of All the Lands.
Therewith, a simpler, purer, larger life,
Unhampered by the dread of war's alarms,
A life attuned to closer touch with Thee,
And golden-threaded with Thy Charity;
A Sweeter Earth, a Nearer Heaven, a World
As emulous in Peace as once in War,
And striving ever upward towards The Goal.

So, once again, through Death shall come New Life,
And out of Darkness, Light.

"POLICEMAN X," which appeared first in Bees in Amber, was written in 1898. The Epilogue was written in 1914. "Policeman X" is the Kaiser. "Policeman" because if he had so chosen he could have assisted in policing Europe and preserving the peace of the world. "X" because he was then the unknown quantity. Now we know him only too well.

THE MEETING-PLACE
(A Warning)

I saw my fellows
In Poverty Street,
Bitter and black with life's defeat,
Ill-fed, ill-housed, of ills complete.
And I said to myself,
"Surely death were sweet

To the people who live in Poverty Street."

I saw my fellows
In Market Place,
Avid and anxious, and hard of face,
Sweating their souls in the Godless race.
And I said to myself,
"How shall these find grace
Who tread Him to death in the Market Place?"

I saw my fellows
In Vanity Fair,
Revelling, rollicking, debonair,
Life all a Gaudy-Show, never a care.
And I said to myself,
"Is there place for these
In my Lord's well-appointed policies?"

I saw my fellows
In Old Church Row,
Hot in discussion of things High and Low,
Cold to the seething volcano below.
And I said to myself,
"The leaven is dead.
The salt has no savour. The Spirit is fled."

I saw my fellows
As men and men,
The Men of Pain, and the Men of Gain,
And the Men who lived in Gallanty-Lane.
And I said to myself,
"What if those should dare
To claim from these others their rightful share?"

I saw them all
Where the Cross-Roads meet;
Vanity Fair, and Poverty Street,
And the Mart, and the Church, when the Red Drums beat,
And summoned them all to The Great Court-Leet.
And I cried unto God,
"Now grant us Thy grace!"

For that was a terrible Meeting-Place.

VICTORY DAY
An Anticipation

As sure as God's in His Heaven,
As sure as He stands for Right,
As sure as the hun this wrong hath done,

So surely we win this fight!

Then!
Then, the visioned eye shall see
The great and noble company,
That gathers there from land and sea,
From over-land and over-sea,
From under-land and under-sea,
To celebrate right royally
The Day of Victory.

Not alone on that great day,
Will the war-worn victors come,
To meet our great glad "Welcome Home!"
And a whole world's deep "Well done!"
Not alone! Not alone will they come,
To the sound of the pipe and the drum;
They will come to their own
With the pipe and the drum,
With the merry merry tune
Of the pipe and the drum;
But-they-will-not-come-alone!

In their unseen myriads there,
Unperceived, but no less there,
In the vast of God's own air,
They will come!
With never a pipe or a drum,
All the flower of Christendom,
In a silence more majestic,
They will come! They will come!
The unknown and the known,
To meet our deep "Well done!"
And the world-resounding thunders
Of our great glad "Welcome Home!"

With their faces all alight,
And their brave eyes shining bright,
From their glorious martyrdom,
They will come!
They will once more all unite
With their comrades of the fight,
To share the world's delight
In the Victory of Right,
And the doom, the final doom
The final, full, and everlasting doom
Of brutal Might,
They will come!

At the world-convulsing boom
Of the treacherous Austrian gun,

At the all-compelling "Come!"
Of that deadly signal-gun,
They gauged the peril, and they came.
Of many a race, and many a name,
But all ablaze with one white flame,
They tarried not to count the cost,
But came.
They came from many a clime and coast,
The slim of limb, the dark of face,
They shouldered eager in the race
The sturdy giants of the frost,
And the stalwarts of the sun,
Britons, Britons, Britons are they!
Britons, every one!
It shall be their life-long boast,
That they counted not the cost,
But, at the Mother-Country's call, they came.
They came a wrong to right,
They came to end the blight
Of a vast ungodly might;
And by their gallant coming overcame.
Britons, Britons, Britons are they!
Britons, every one!

It shall be their nobler boast,
It shall spell their endless fame,
That, regardless of the cost,
They won the world for Righteousness,
And cleansed it of its shame.
Britons, Britons, Britons are they!
Britons, every one!

And now, again they come,
With merry pipe and drum,
Amid the storming cheers,
And the grateful-streaming tears,
Of this our great, glad, sorrowing Welcome-Home.
They shall every one be there,
On the earth or in the air,
From the land and from the sea,
And from under-land and sea,
Not a man shall missing be
From the past and present fighting-strength
Of that great company.
Those who lived, and those who died,
They were one in noble pride
Of desperate endeavour and of duty nobly done;
For their lives they risked and gave
Very Soul of Life to save,
And by their own great valour, and the Grace of God, they won.
Britons, Britons, Britons are they!

Britons, every one!

As gold is tried in the furnace,
So He tries the hearts of men;
And the dwale and the dross shall suffer loss,
When He tries the hearts of men.
And the wood, and the hay, and the stubble
Shall pass in the flame away,
For gain is loss, and loss is gain,
And treasure of earth is poor and vain,
When He tries the hearts of men.

As gold is refined in the furnace,
So He fines the hearts of men.
The purge of the flame doth rid them of shame,
When He tries the hearts of men.
O, better than gold, yea, than much fine gold,
When He tries the hearts of men,
Are Faith, and Hope, and Truth, and Love,
And the Wisdom that cometh from above,
When He tries the hearts of men.

POISON-SEEDS
Is there, in you or me,
Seed of that poison-tree
Which, in its bitter fruiting, bore
Such vintage sore
Of red calamity
Black wine of horror and of Death,
And soul-catastrophe?
Search well and see!

Yea search and see!
And, if there be
Tear up its roots with zealous care,
With deep soul-probing and with prayer,
Lest, in the coming years,
Again it bear
This same dread fruit of blood and tears,
And ruth beyond compare.

Each soul that strips it of one evil thing
Lifts all the world towards God's good purposing.

THE WAR-MAKERS
Who are the Makers of Wars?

The Kings of the earth.

And who are these Kings of the earth?
Only men not always even men of worth,
But claiming rule by right of birth.

And Wisdom? does that come by birth?
Nay then too often the reverse.
Wise father oft has son perverse;
Solomon's son was Israel's curse.

Why suffer things to reason so averse?
It always has been so,
And only now does knowledge grow
To that high point where all men know
Who would be free must strike the blow.

And how long will man suffer so?
Until his soul of Freedom sings,
And, strengthened by his sufferings,
He breaks the worn-out leading-strings,
And calls to stricter reckonings
Those costliest things unworthy Kings.

Not all are worthless. Some, with sense of duty,
Strive to invest their lives with grace and beauty.
To such high honour! But the rest, self-seekers,
Pride-puffed, out with them! useless mischief-makers!

The time is past when any man or nation
Will meekly bear unrighteous domination.

The time is come when every burden-bearer
Must, in the fixing of his load, be sharer.

IS LIFE WORTH LIVING?
Is life worth living?
It depends on your believing;
If it ends with this short span,
Then is man no better than
The beasts that perish.
But a Loftier Hope we cherish.
"Life out of Death" is written wide
Across Life's page on every side.
We cannot think as ended, our dear dead who died.

What room is left us then for doubt or fear?
Love laughs at thought of ending there, or here.
God would lack meaning if this world were all,
And this short life but one long funeral.

God is! Christ loves! Christ lives!
And by His Own Returning gives
Sure pledge of Immortality.
The first-fruits He; and we
The harvest of His victory.
The life beyond shall this life far transcend,
And Death is the Beginning not the End!

GOD'S HANDWRITING

He writes in characters too grand
For our short sight to understand;
We catch but broken strokes, and try
To fathom all the mystery
Of withered hopes, of death, of life,
The endless war, the useless strife,
But there, with larger, clearer sight,
We shall see this

HIS WAY WAS RIGHT

(From Bees in Amber.)

PART TWO: THE KING'S HIGH WAY

THE KING'S HIGH WAY

A wonderful Way is The King's High Way;
It runs through the Nightlands up to the Day;
From the wonderful WAS, by the wonderful IS,
To the still more wonderful IS TO BE,
Runs The King's High Way.

Through the crooked by-ways of history,
Through the times that were dark with mystery,
From the cities of man's captivity,
By the shed of The Child's nativity,
And over the hill by the crosses three,
By the sign-post of God's paternity,
From Yesterday into Eternity,
Runs The King's High Way.
And wayfaring men, who have strayed, still say
It is good to travel The King's High Way.

Through the dim, dark Valley of Death, at times,
To the peak of the Shining Mount it climbs,
While wonders, and glories, and joys untold
To the eyes of the visioned each step unfold,
On The King's High Way.

And everywhere there are sheltering bowers,
Plenished with fruits and radiant with flowers,
Where the weary of body and soul may rest,
As the steeps they breast to the beckoning crest,
On The King's High Way.

And inns there are too, of comforting mien,
Where every guest is a King or a Queen,
And room never lacks in the inns on that road,
For the hosts are all gentle men, like unto God,
On The King's High Way.

The comrades one finds are all bound the same way,
Their faces aglow in the light of the day;
And never a quarrel is heard, nor a brawl,
They're the best of good company, each one and all,
On The King's High Way.

So, gallantly travel The King's High Way,
With hearts unperturbed and with souls high and gay,
There is many a road that is much more the mode,
But none that so surely leads straight up to God,
As The King's High Way.

THE WAYS

To every man there openeth
A Way, and Ways, and a Way,
And the High Soul climbs the High Way,
And the Low Soul gropes the Low,
And in between, on the misty flats,
The rest drift to and fro.
But to every man there openeth
A High Way, and a Low.
And every man decideth
The Way his soul shall go.

AD FINEM

Britain! Our Britain! uprisen in the splendour
Of your white wrath at treacheries so vile;
Roused from your sleep, become once more defender
Of those high things which make life worth life's while!

Now, God be thanked for even such a wakening
From the soft dreams of peace in selfish ease,
If it but bring about the great heart-quickening,
Of which are born the larger liberties.

Ay, better such a rousing up from slumber;
Better this fight for His High Empery;

Better e'en though our fair sons without number
Pave with their lives the road to victory.

But Britain! Britain! What if it be written,
On the great scrolls of Him who holds the ways,
That to the dust the foe shall not be smitten
Till unto Him we pledge redeemèd days?

Till unto Him we turn in deep soul-sorrow,
For all the past that was so stained and dim,
For all the present ills and for a morrow
Founded and built and consecrated to Him.

Take it to heart! This ordeal has its meaning;
By no fell chance has such a horror come.
Take it to heart! nor count indeed on winning,
Until the lesson has come surely home.

Take it to heart! nor hope to find assuagement
Of this vast woe, until, with souls subdued,
Stripped of all less things, in most high engagement,
We seek in Him the One and Only Good.

Not of our own might shall this tribulation
Pass, and once more to earth be peace restored;
Not till we turn, in solemn consecration,
Wholly to Him, our One and Sovereign Lord.

EVENING BRINGS US HOME
Evening brings us home,
From our wanderings afar,
From our multifarious labours,
From the things that fret and jar;
From the highways and the byways,
From the hill-tops and the vales;
From the dust and heat of city street,
And the joys of lonesome trails,
Evening brings us home at last,
To Thee.

From plough and hoe and harrow, from the burden of the day,
From the long and lonely furrow in the stiff reluctant clay,
From the meads where streams are purling,
From the moors where mists are curling,
Evening brings us home at last,
To rest, and warmth, and Thee.

From the pastures where the white lambs to their dams are ever crying,
From the byways where the Night lambs Thy
Love are crucifying,

From the labours of the lowlands,
From the glamour of the glowlands,
Evening brings us home at last,
To the fold, and rest, and Thee.

From the Forests of Thy Wonder, where the mighty giants grow,
Where we cleave Thy works asunder, and lay the mighty low,
From the jungle and the prairie,
From the realms of fact and faerie,
Evening brings us home at last,
To rest, and cheer, and Thee.

From our wrestlings with the spectres of the dim and dreary way,
From the vast heroic chances of the never-ending fray,
From the Mount of High Endeavour,
In the hope of Thy For Ever,
Evening brings us home at last,
To trust and peace, and Thee.

From our toilings and our moilings, from the quest of daily bread,
From the worship of our idols, and the burying of our dead,
Like children, worn and weary
With the way so long and dreary,
Evening brings us home at last,
To rest, and love, and Thee.

From our journeyings oft and many over strange and stormy seas,
From our search the wide world over for the larger liberties,
From our labours vast and various,
With our harvestings precarious,
Evening brings us home at last,
To safety, rest, and Thee.

From the yet-untrodden No-Lands, where we sought Thy secrets out,
From the blizzards of the Nightlands, and the
blazing White-Lands' drought,
From the undiscovered country
Where our IS is yet to be,
Evening brings us home at last,
To welcome cheer, and Thee.

From the temples of our living, all empurpled with Thy giving,
From the warp of life thick-threaded with the gold of Thine inweaving,
From the days so full of splendour,
From the visions rare and tender,
Evening brings us home at last,
To quiet rest in Thee.

From the Dim-Lands, from the Grim-Lands,
from the Lands of High Emprise,
From the Lands of Disillusion to the Truth that never dies;

With rejoicing and with singing,
Each his rightful sheaves home-bringing,
Evening brings us all at last,
To Harvest-Home with Thee.

From the fields of fiery trying, where our bravest and our best,
By their living and their dying their souls' high faith attest,
From these dread, red fields of sorrow,
From the fight for Thy To-morrow,
Evening brings each one at last,
To GOD'S own Peace in Thee.

THE REAPER

All through the blood-red Autumn,
When the harvest came to the full;
When the days were sweet with sunshine,
And the nights were wonderful,
The Reaper reaped without ceasing.

All through the roaring Winter,
When the skies were black with wrath,
When earth alone slept soundly,
And the seas were white with froth,
The Reaper reaped without ceasing.

All through the quick of the Spring-time,
When the birds sang cheerily,
When the trees and the flowers were burgeoning,
And men went wearily,
The Reaper reaped without ceasing.

All through the blazing Summer,
When the year was at its best,
When Earth, subserving God alone,
In her fairest robes was dressed,
The Reaper reaped without ceasing.

So, through the Seasons' roundings,
While nature waxed and waned,
And only man by thrall of man
Was scarred and marred and stained,
The Reaper reaped without ceasing.

How long, O Lord, shall the Reaper
Harry the growing field?
Stretch out Thy Hand and stay him,
Lest the future no fruit yield!
And the Gleaner find nought for His gleaning.

Thy Might alone can end it,

This fratricidal strife.
Our souls are sick with the tale of death,
Redeem us back to life!
That the Gleaner be glad in His gleaning.

NO MAN GOETH ALONE

Where one is,
There am I,
No man goeth alone!

Though he fly to earth's remotest bound,
Though his soul in the depths of sin be drowned,
No man goeth alone!

Though he take him the wings of fear, and flee
Past the outermost realms of light;
Though he weave him a garment of mystery,
And hide in the womb of night,
No man goeth alone!

Though apart in the city's heart he dwell,
Though he wander beyond the stars,
Though he bury himself in his nethermost hell,
And vanish behind the bars,
No man goeth alone!

For I, God, am the soul of man,
And none can Me dethrone.
Where one is,
There am I,
No man goeth alone!

ROSEMARY

Singing, she washed
Her baby's clothes,
And, one by one,
As they were done,
She hung them in the sun to dry,
She hung them on a bush hard by,
Upon a waiting bush hard by,
A glad expectant bush hard by,
To dry in the sweet of the morning.

The while, her son,
Her little son,
Lay kicking, gleeful,
In the sun,
Her little, naked, Virgin son.

O wondrous sight! Amazing sight!
The Lord, who did the sun create,
Lay kicking with a babe's delight,
Regardless of His low estate,
In joy of nakedness elate,
In His own sun's fair light!

And all the sweet, sweet, sweet of Him
Clave to the bush, and still doth cleave,
And doth forever-more outgive
The fragrant holy sweet of Him.
Where'er it thrives
That bush forthgives
The faint, rare, sacred sweet of Him.

So ever sweet, and ever green,
Shall Rosemary be queen.

EASTER SUNDAY, 1916
The sun shone white and fair,
This Eastertide,
Yet all its sweetness seemed but to deride
Our souls' despair;
For stricken hearts, and loss and pain,
Were everywhere.
We sang our Alleluias,
We said, "The Christ is risen!
From this His earthly prison,
The Christ indeed is risen.
He is gone up on high,
To the perfect peace of heaven."

Then, with a sigh,
We wondered...
Our minds evolved grim hordes of huns,
Our bruised hearts sank beneath the guns,
On our very souls they thundered.
Can you wonder? Can you wonder,
That we wondered,
As we heard the huns' guns thunder?
That we looked in one another's eyes
And wondered,

"Is Christ indeed then risen from the dead?
Hath He not rather fled
For ever from a world where He
Meets such contumely?"

Our hearts were sick with pain,
As they beat the sad refrain,

"How shall the Lord Christ come again?
How can the Lord Christ come again?
Nay, will He come again?
Is He not surely fled
For ever from a world where He
Is still so buffeted?"

But the day's glory all forbade
Such depth of woe. Came to our aid
The sun, the birds, the springing things,
The winging things, the singing things;
And taught us this,
After each Winter cometh Spring,
God's hand is still in everything,
His mighty purposes are sure,
His endless love doth still endure,
And will not cease, nor know remiss,
Despite man's forfeiture.

The Lord is risen indeed!
In very truth and deed
The Lord is risen, is risen, is risen;
He will supply our need.

So we took heart again,
And built us refuges from pain
Within His coverture,
Strong towers of Love, and Hope, and Faith,
That shall maintain
Our souls' estate
Too high and great
For even Death to violate.

THE CHILD OF THE MAID
On Christmas Day The Child was born,
On Christmas Day in the morning;
To tread the long way, lone and lorn,
To wear the bitter crown of thorn,
To break the heart by man's sins torn,
To die at last the Death of Scorn.
For this The Child of The Maid was born,
On Christmas Day in the morning.

But that first day when He was born,
Among the cattle and the corn,
The sweet Maid-Mother wondering,
And sweetly, deeply, pondering
The words that in her heart did ring,
Unto her new-born king did sing,

"My baby, my baby,
My own little son,
Whence come you,
Where go you,
My own little one?
Whence come you?

Ah now, unto me all alone
That wonder of wonders is properly known.
Where go you?
Ah, that now, 'tis only He knows,
Who sweetly on us, dear, such favour bestows.
In us, dear, this day is some great work begun,
Ah me, little son dear, I would it were done!
I wonder ... I wonder ...
And-wish-it-were-done!

"O little, little feet, dears.
So curly, curly sweet!
How will it be with you, dears,
When all your work's complete?
O little, little hands, dears,
That creep about my breast!
What great things you will do, dears,
Before you lie at rest!
O softest little head, dear,
It shall have crown of gold,
For it shall have great honour
Before the world grows old!
O sweet, white, soft round body,
It shall sit upon a throne!
My little one, my little one,
Thou art the Highest's son!
All this the angel told me,
And so I'm sure it's true,
For he told me who was coming,
And that sweet thing is YOU."

On Christmas Day The Child was born,
On Christmas Day in the morning;
He trod the long way, lone and lorn,
He wore the bitter crown of thorn,
His hands and feet and heart were torn,
He died at last the Death of Scorn.
But through His coming Death was slain,
That you and I might live again.

For this The Child of The Maid was born,
On Christmas Day in the morning.

WASTED?

Think not of any one of them as wasted,
Or to the void like broken tools outcasted,
Unnoticed, unregretted, and unknown.
Not so is His care shown.

Know this!
In God's economy there is no waste,
As in His Work no slackening, no haste;
But noiselessly, without a sign,
The measure of His vast design
Is all fulfilled, exact as He hath willed.

And His good instruments He tends with care,
Lest aught their future usefulness impair,
As Master-craftsman his choice tools doth tend,
Respecting each one as a trusty friend,
Cleans them, and polishes, and puts away,
For his good usage at some future day;
So He unto Himself has taken these,
Not to their loss but to their vast increase.
To us, the loss, the emptiness, the pain;
But unto them all high eternal gain.

SHORTENED LIVES

To us it seemed his life was too soon done,
Ended, indeed, while scarcely yet begun;
God, with His clearer vision, saw that he
Was ready for a larger ministry.

Just so we thought of Him, whose life below
Was so full-charged with bitterness and woe,
Our clouded vision would have crowned Him King,
He chose the lowly way of suffering.

Remember, too, how short His life on earth,
But three-and-thirty years 'twixt death and birth.
And of those years but three whereof we know,
Yet those three years immortal seed did sow.

It is not tale of years that tells the whole
Of Man's success or failure, but the soul
He brings to them, the songs he sings to them,
The steadfast gaze he fixes on the goal.

LAGGARD SPRING

Winter hung about the ways,
Very loth to go.
Little Spring could not get past him,

Try she never so.

This side, that side, everywhere,
Winter held the track.
Little Spring sat down and whimpered,
Winter humped his back.

Summer called her, "Come, dear, come!
Why do you delay?"
"Come and help me, Sister Summer,
Winter blocks my way."

Little Spring tried everything,
Sighs and moans and tears,
Winter howled with mocking laughter,
Covered her with jeers.

Winter, rough old surly beggar,
Practised every vice,
Pelted her with hail and snow storms,
Clogged her feet with ice.

But, by chance at last they caught him
Unawares one day,
Tied his hands and feet, and dancing,
Sped upon their way.

LONELY BROTHER
Art thou lonely, O my brother?
Share thy little with another!
Stretch a hand to one unfriended,
And thy loneliness is ended.
So both thou and he
Shall less lonely be.
And of thy one loneliness
Shall come two's great happiness.

COMFORT YE!
"Comfort ye, my people!"
Saith your God,
"And be ye comforted!
And-be-ye-comforted!"

Roughly my plough did plough you,
Sharp were my strokes, and sore,
But nothing less could bow you,
Nothing less could your souls restore
To the depths and the heights of my longing,
To the strength you had known before.

For you were falling, falling,
Even the best of you,
Falling from your high calling;
And this, My test of you,
Has been for your souls' redemption
From the little things of earth,
What seemed to you death's agony
Was but a greater birth.

And now you shall have gladness
For the years you have seen ill;
Give up to Me your sadness,
And I your cup will fill.

S. ELIZABETH'S LEPER

"My lord, there came unto the gate
One, in such pitiful estate,
So all forlorn and desolate,
Ill-fed, ill-clad, of ills compact;
A leper too, his poor flesh wracked
And dead, his very bones infect;
Of all God's sons none so abject.
I could not, on the Lord's own day,
Turn such a stricken one away.
In pity him I took, and fed,
And happed him in our royal bed."

"A leper! in our bed! Nay then,
My Queen, thy charities do pass
The bounds of sense at times! A bane
On such unwholesome tenderness!
Dost nothing owe to him who shares
Thy couch, and suffers by thy cares?
He could have slept upon the floor,
And left you still his creditor.
A leper! in my bed! God's truth!
Out upon such outrageous ruth!"

He strode in anger towards the bed,
And lo!
The Christ, with thorn-crowned head,
Lay there in sweet sleep pillowed.

VOX CLAMANTIS

(THE PLEA OF THE MUNITION-WORKER)
"Rattle and clatter and clank and whirr,"
And it's long and long the day is.
From earliest morn to late at night,

And all night long, the selfsame song,
"Rattle and clank and whirr."
Day in, day out, all day, all night,
"Rattle and clank and whirr;"
With faces tight, with all our might,
"Rattle and clank and whirr;"
We may not stop and we dare not err;
Our men are risking their lives out there,
And we at home must do our share;
But it's long and long the day is.
We'll break if we must, but we cannot spare
A thought for ourselves, or the kids, or care,
For it's "Rattle and clatter and clank and whirr;"
Our men are giving their lives out there
And we'll give ours, we will do our share,
"Rattle and clank and whirr."

Are our faces grave, and our eyes intent?
Is every ounce that is in us bent
On the uttermost pitch of accomplishment?
Though it's long and long the day is!
Ah we know what it means if we fool or slack;
A rifle jammed, and one comes not back;
And we never forget, it's for us they gave;
And so we will slave, and slave, and slave,
Lest the men at the front should rue it.
Their all they gave, and their lives we'll save,
If the hardest of work can do it;
But it's long and long the day is.

Eight hours', ten hours', twelve hours' shift;
Oh, it's long and long the day is!
Up before light, and home in the night,
That is our share in the desperate fight;
And it's long and long the day is!
Backs and arms and heads that ache,
Eyes over-tired and legs that shake,
And hearts full nigh to burst and break;
Oh, it's long and long the day is!
Week in, week out, not a second to spare,
But though it should kill us we'll do our share,
For the sake of the lads, who have gone out there
For the sake of us others, to do and dare;
But it's long and long the day is!

"Rattle and clatter and clank and whirr,"
And thousands of wheels a-spinning,
Spinning Death for the men of wrath,
Spinning Death for the broken troth,
And Life, and a New Beginning.
Was there ever, since ever the world was made,

Such a horrible trade for a peace-loving maid,
And such wonderful, terrible spinning?

Oh, it's dreary work and it's weary work,
But none of us all will fall or shirk.

FLORA'S BIT

Flora, with wondrous feathers in her hat,
Rain-soaked, and limp, and feeling very flat,
With flowers of sorts in her full basket, sat,
Back to the railings, there by Charing Cross,
And cursed the weather and a blank day's loss.

"Wevver!" she cried, to P. C. E. 09,
"Wevver, you calls it? Your sort then, not mine!
I calls it blanky 'NO.' So there you are,
Bit of Old Nick's worstest particular.
Wevver indeed! Not much, my little son,
It's just old London's nastiest kind of fun.

"Vi'lets, narcissus, primroses and daffs,
See how they sits up in their beds an' laughs!
Buy, Pretty Ladies for your next at 'ome!
Gents! for the gells now buy a pretty bloom!

"Gosh! but them 'buses is a fair disgrace,
Squirting their dirty mud into one's face,
Robert, my son, you a'n't half worth your salt,
Or you'd arrest 'em for a blank assault!

"Primroses, narcissus, daffs and violets,
First come is first served, and pick o' basket gets.

"Garn then and git! Ain't none o' you no good!
Cawn't spare a copper to'rds a pore gell's food.
Gives one the 'ump it does, to see you all go by,
An' me a-sittin' 'ere all day,
An' none o' you won't buy.
Vi'lets, narcissus, ... Blimy! Strike me dumb!
Garn! What's the good o' you? lot o' dirty scum!
Silly blokes! stony brokes! I'm a-goin' 'ome!"

And then, from out the "Corner-House,"
Came two, and two, and two,
Three pretty maids, three little Subs,
Doing as young Subs do,
When four days' leave gives them the chance
Of a little bill and coo.

"What ho!" they cried, as they espied

Flora's bright flower-pot.
"Hi! you there with the last year's hat!
Let's see what you have got!
And if they're half as nice as you,
We'll buy the blooming lot."

But, as they stood there chaffering,
Out from the station came
A string of cautious motor-cars,
Packed full of lean, brown men,
The halt, the maimed, the blind, the lame,
The wreckage of the wars,
Their faces pinched and full of pain,
Their eyes still dazed with stress and strain,
The nation's creditors.

The Subs, the girls, and Flora stood,
There in the pouring rain,
And shouted hearty welcomes to
The broken, lean-faced men.
And when they'd passed, the little Subs
Turned to their fun again.

But the biggest heart among them all
Beat under the feathered hat;
"Not me!" she cried, and up, and sped
After the boys who had fought and bled,
"Here's a game worth two o' that!"

She caught the cars, and in she flung
Her wares with lavish hand.
"Narcissus! vi'lets! here, you chaps!
Primroses! dafs! for your rumply caps!
My! Ain't you black-an'-tanned!
Narcissus! vi'lets! all abloom,
We're glad to see you back.
Primroses! dafs! Thenk Gawd you laughs,
If it's on'y crooked smiles.
We're glad, my lads, to see you home,
If your faces are like files."

They thanked her with their crooked smiles,
Their bandaged hands they waved,
Narcissus, vi'lets, prims, and daffs,
They welcomed them with twisted laughs,
Quite proper they behaved.
And one said, "You're a Daisy, dear,
And if you'd stop the 'bus
We'd every one give you a kiss,
And so say all of us.
A Daisy, dear, that's what you are."

And the rest, "You are! You are!"

Then Flora swung her basket high,
And tossed her feathered head;
To the boys she gave one final wave,
And to herself she said,
"What kind of a silly old fool am I,
Playin' the goat like that?
Chuckin' of all my stock awye,
And damaging me 'at?
But them poor lads did look so thin,
I couldn't ha' slept if I 'adn't a-bin
An' gone an' done this foolish thing.
An' it done them good, an' it done me good,
So what's the odds if I does go lean,
For a day or two, till the nibs comes in?
A gell like me can always live,
An' the bit I had I had to give.
An' he called me a Daisy! Aw, 'Daisy dear!'
An' I tell you, it made me queer,
With a lump in me throat and a swell right here.
Fust time ever any one called me that,
An', I swear, it's better'n a bran new hat."

RED BREAST
I saw one hanging on a tree,
And O his face was sad to see,
Misery, misery me!

There were berries red upon his head,
And in his hands, and on his feet,
But when I tried to pick and eat,
They were his blood, and he was dead;
Misery, misery me!

It broke my heart to see him there,
So lone and sad in his despair;
The nails of woe were through his hands,
And through his feet, ah, misery me!

With beak and claws I did my best
To loose the nails and set him free,
But they were all too strong for me;
Misery, misery me!

I picked and pulled, and did my best,
And his red blood stained all my breast;
I bit the nails, I pecked the thorn,
O, never saw I thorn so worn;
But yet I could not get him free;

Misery, misery me!

And never since have I feared man,
But ever I seek him when I can,
And let him see the wish in me
To ease him of his misery.

OUR HEARTS FOR YOU

By the grace of God and the courage
Of the peoples far and wide,
By the toil and sweat of those who lived,
And the blood of those who died,
We have won the fight, we have saved the Right,
For the Lord was on our side.

We have come through the valley of shadows,
We have won to the light again,
We have smitten to earth the evil thing,
And our sons have proved them men.
But not alone by our might have we won,
For the Lord fought in our van.

When the night was at its darkest,
And never a light could we see,
When earth seemed like to be enslaved
In a monstrous tyranny;
Then the flaming sword of our Over-Lord
Struck home for liberty.

All the words in the world cannot tell you
What brims in our hearts for you;
For the lives you gave our lives to save
We offer our hearts to you;
We can never repay, we can only pray,
God fulfil our hearts for you!

THE BURDENED ASS
(AN ALLEGORY)

One day, as I travelled the highway alone,
I heard, on in front, a most dolorous groan;
And there, round the corner, a weary old ass
Was nuzzling the hedge for a mouthful of grass.
The load that he carried was piled up so high
That it blocked half the road and threatened the sky.
Indeed, of himself I could see but a scrap,
And expected each minute to see that go snap;
For beneath all his load I could see but his legs,
And they were as thin as the thinnest clothes-pegs.

I said, "O most gentle and innocent beast,
Say, why is your burden so greatly increased?
Who loads you like this, beyond reason and right?
Is it done for a purpose, or just out of spite?
Is it all your own treasures you have in your pack,
That crumples your backbone and makes your ribs crack?
It is really too much for an old ass's back."

"Treasures!" he groaned, through a lump of chewed grass,
"Are they treasures? I don't know. I'm only the ass
That carries whatever they all like to pack
On my load, without thought of my ribs or my back.
I know there are heaps of things there that I hate,
But it's always been so. I guess it's my fate."
And he flicked his long ears, and switched his thin tail,
And rasped his rough neck with a hinder-foot nail.

"There are fighting-men somewhere up there, and some fools,
And talking-men, heaps, who have quitted their stools
To manage the state and direct its affairs,
And see, I suppose, that we all get our shares,
And ladies and lords, and their offspring and heirs,
And their flunkeys and toadies, and merchants and wares.
And parsons and lawyers, O heaps, in that box,
And big folk and small folk, and all kinds of crocks.

"That mighty big bale? Poison, that, for the people;
Whatever else lacks they must still have their tipple.
That's The Trade, don't you know, that no one can shackle,
'Vested Int'rests,' they call it, and that kind of cackle.
Why the Bishops themselves dare not tackle the tipple,
For it props up the church and at times builds a steeple."

(A strangely ingenuous old ass, you perceive,
Whom any shrewd rascal could easily deceive.)

"That other big bale? What I said, fighting things,
Ammunition and guns and these new things with wings,
O yes, they bulk big, but we need them, for why?
If we hadn't as much as the others have why,
They say we might just as well lie down and die.

"Yon big bale on top? Ah! that is a big weight.
And that's just the one of the lot I most hate.
That's Capital, that is, and landlords and such;
And there seems to me sometimes a bit over-much
In that bale. But there, I'm perhaps wrong again,
Such matters are outside an old ass's ken.

"My fodder? Oh well, you see, no room for that.
I pick as I go, and no chance to get fat.

That poison bulks large, and the landlords, you see;
And that Capital's heavy as heavy can be.
Some one's bound to go short, and of course that one's ME."

He kicked up one heel with a snort of disgust,
And sudden as though by a giant hand thrust,
The top-heavy pack on his lean back revolved,
Came crashing to earth, and in fragments dissolved.

Much surprised, the old ass, thus set free from his load,
Picked out a soft spot in the nice dusty road,
And laid him down on it and rolled in high glee,
And, as he kicked this way and that, said to me,

"Say, Man, I have never enjoyed such a roll
Since the day I was born, a silly young foal.
Seems to me, if I'd had half the sense of an ass,
I'd have long since got rid of that troublesome mass.
But now that it's down, why down it shall stop.
All my life's been down under, but now I'm on top."

Then he came right-side up, pranced about on his load,
And kicked it to pieces all over the road.

And what all this means, I really can't say.
It may not mean much. But again, why, it may.

WINNERS OR LOSERS?
Unless our Souls win back to Thee,
We shall have lost this fight.
Yes, though we win on field and sea,
Though mightier still our might may be,
We still shall lose if we win not Thee.
Help us to climb, as in Thy sight,
The Great High Way of Thy Delight.

It is the world-old strife again,
The fight 'twixt good and ill.
Since first the curse broke out in Cain,
Each age has worn the grim red chain,
And ill fought good for sake of gain.
Help us, through all life's conflict, still
To battle upwards to Thy Will.

Are we to be like all the rest,
Or climb we loftier height?
Can we our wayward steps arrest?
All life with nobler life invest?
And so fulfil our Lord's behest?
Help us, through all the world's dark night,

To struggle upwards to the Light.

If not, we too shall pass, as passed
The older peoples in their time.
God's pact is sure, His word stands fast,
Those who His sovereignty outcast
Outcast themselves shall be at last.
So, lest we pass in this our prime,
Lord, set us to the upward climb!

CHRIST AT THE BAR

Christ stands at the bar of the world to-day,
As He stood in the days of old.
And still, as then, we do betray
Our Lord for greed of gold.

When our every deed and word and thought
Should our fealty proclaim,
Full oft we bring His name to nought
And cover Him with shame.

Not alone did Judas his Master sell,
Nor Peter his Lord deny,
Each one who doth His love repel,
Or at His guidance doth rebel,
Doth the Lord Christ crucify.

Like the men of old, we vote His death,
Lest His life should interfere
With the things we have, or the things we crave,
Or the things we hold more dear.

Christ stands at the bar of the world to-day,
As He stood in the days of old.
Let each man tax his soul and say,
"Shall I again my Lord betray
For my greed, or my goods, or my gold?"

MY BROTHER'S KEEPER?
(A WARNING)

"Am I my brother's keeper?"
Yes, of a truth!
Thine asking is thine answer.
That self-condemning cry of Cain
Has been the plea of every selfish soul since then,
Which hath its brother slain.
God's word is plain,
And doth thy shrinking soul arraign.

Thy brother's keeper?
Yea, of a truth thou art!
For if not who?
Are ye not both, both thou and he
Of God's great family?
How rid thee of thy soul's responsibility?
For every ill in all the world
Each soul is sponsor and account must bear.
And He, and he thy brother of despair,
Claim, of thy overmuch, their share.

Thou hast had good, and he the strangled days;
But now, the old things pass.
No longer of thy grace
Is he content to live in evil case
For the anointing of thy shining face.
The old things pass. Beware lest ye pass with them,
And your place
Become an emptiness!

Beware! Lest, when the "Have-nots" claim,
From those who have, their rightful share,
Thy borders be swept bare
As by the final flame.
Better to share before than after.
"After?" ... For thee may be no after!
Only the howl of mocking laughter
At thy belated care. Make no mistake!
"After" will be too late.
When once the "Have-nots" claim ... they take.
"After!" ... When that full claim is made,
You and your golden gods may all lie dead.

Set now your house in order,
Ere it be too late!
For, once the storm of hate
Be loosed, no man shall stay it till
Its thirst has slaked its fill,
And you, poor victims of this last "too late,"
Shall in the shadows mourn your lost estate.

A TELEPHONE MESSAGE
(TO WHOM IT MAY CONCERN)
Hello! Hello!
Are you there? Are you there?
Ah! That you? Well,
This is just to tell you
That there's trouble in the air...
Trouble,
T-R-O-U-B-L-E Trouble!

Where?
In the air.
Trouble in the air!
Got that? ... Right!
Then take a word of warning,
And ... Beware!

What trouble?
Every trouble, everywhere,
Every wildest kind of nightmare
That has ridden you is there,
In the air.
And it's coming like a whirlwind,
Like a wild beast mad with hunger,
To rend and wrench and tear,
To tear the world in pieces maybe,
Unless it gets its share.
Can't you see the signs and portents?
Can't you feel them in the air?
Can't you see, you unbeliever?
Can't you see? or don't you care,
That the Past is gone for ever,
Past your uttermost endeavour,
That To-day is on the scrap-heap,
And the Future anywhere?

Where?
Ah that's beyond me!
But it lies with those who dare
To think of big To-morrows,
And intend to have their share.

All the things you've held and trusted
Are played-out, decayed, and rusted;
Now, in fiery circumstance,
They will all be readjusted.
If you cling to those old things,
Hoping still to hold the strings,
And, for your ungodly gains,
Life to bind with golden chains;
Man! you're mightily mistaken!
From such dreams you'd best awaken
To the sense of what is coming,
When you hear the low, dull booming
Of the far-off tocsin drums.
Such a day of vast upsettings,
Dire outcastings and downsettings!
You have held the reins too long,
Have you time to heal the wrong?

What's wrong? What's amiss?

Man alive! If you don't know that
There's nothing more to be said!
You ask what's amiss when your destinies
Hang by a thread in the great abyss?
What's amiss? What's amiss?
Well, my friend, just this,
There's a bill to pay and it's due to-day,
And before it's paid you may all be dead.
Wake up! Wake up! or, all too late,
You will find yourselves exterminate.

What's wrong?
Listen here!
Do you catch a sound like drumming?
Far-away and distant drumming?
You hear it? What?
The wires humming?
No, my friend, it is not!
It's the tune the prentice-hands are thrumming,
The tune of the dire red time that's coming,
The far-away, pregnant, ghostly booming
Of the great red drums' dread drumming.
For they're coming, coming, coming,
With their dread and doomful drumming,
Unless you...
Br-r-r-r-r-r-r-r-r-click-clack!

THE STARS' ACCUSAL
How can the makers of unrighteous wars
Stand the accusal of the watchful stars?

To stand
A dust-speck, facing the infinitudes
Of Thine unfathomable dome, a night like this,
To stand full-face to Thy High Majesties,
Thy myriad worlds in solemn watchfulness,
Watching, watching, watching all below,
And man in all his wilfulness for woe!
Dear Lord, one wonders that Thou bearest still
With man on whom Thou didst such grace bestow,
And with his wilful faculty for woe!

Those sleepless sentinels! They may be worlds
All peopled like our own. But, as I stand,
They are to me the myriad eyes of God,
Watching, watching, watching all below,
And man in all his wilfulness for woe.
And then to think
What those same piercing eyes look down upon
Elsewhere on this fair earth that Thou hast made!

Watching, watching, watching all below,
And man in all his wilfulness for woe.

On all the desolations he hath wrought,
On all the passioned hatreds he hath taught,
On all Thy great hopes he hath brought to nought;
Man rending man with ruthless bitterness,
Blasting Thine image into nothingness,
Hounding Thy innocents to awful deaths,
And worse than deaths! Happy the dead, who sped
Before the torturers their lust had fed!
On Thy Christ crucified afresh each day,
On all the horrors of War's grim red way.
And ever, in Thy solemn midnight skies,
Those myriad, sleepless, vast accusing eyes,
Watching, watching, watching all below,
And man in all his wilfulness for woe.

Dear Lord!
When in our troubled hearts we ponder this,
We can but wonder at Thy wrath delayed,
We can but wonder that Thy hand is stayed,
We can but wonder at Thy sufferance
Of man, whom Thou in Thine own image made,
When he that image doth so sore degrade!

If Thou shouldst blot us out without a word,
Our stricken souls must say we had incurred
Just punishment.
Warnings we lacked not, warnings oft and clear,
But in our arrogance we gave no ear
To Thine admonishment.
And yet, and yet! O Lord, we humbly pray,
Put back again Thy righteous Judgment Day!
Have patience with us yet a while, until
Through these our sufferings we learn Thy Will.

NO PEACE BUT A RIGHT PEACE
An inconclusive peace!
A peace that would be no peace
Naught but a treacherous truce for breeding
Of a later, greater, baser-still betrayal!
"No!" ...
The spirits of our myriad valiant dead,
Who died to make peace sure and life secure,
Thunder one mighty cry of righteous indignation,
One vast imperative, unanswerable "No!" ...
"Not for that, not for that, did we die!"
They cry;
"To give fresh life to godless knavery!

To forge again the chains of slavery
Such as humanity has never known!
We gave our lives to set Life free,
Loyally, willingly gave we,
Lest on our children, and on theirs,
Should come like misery.
And now, from our souls' heights and depths,
We cry to you, "Beware,
Lest you defraud us of one smallest atom of the price
Of this our sacrifice!
One fraction less than that full liberty,
Which comes of righteous and enduring peace,
Will be betrayal of your trust,
Betrayal of your race, the world, and God."

IN CHURCH. 1916

Where are all the young men?
There are only grey-heads here.
What has become of the young men?

This is the young men's year!
They are gone, one and all, at duty's call,
To the camp, to the trench, to the sea.
They have left their homes, they have left their all,
And now, in ways heroical,
They are making history.
From bank and shop, from bench and mill,
From the schools, from the tail of the plough,
They hurried away at the call of the fray,
They could not linger a day, and now,
They are making history,
And we miss them sorely, as we look
At the seats where they used to be,
And try to picture them as they are,
Then hastily drop the vail: for, you see,
They are making history.

And history, in these dread days,
Is sore sore sad in the making;
We are building the future with our dead,
We are binding it sure with the brave blood shed,
Though our hearts are well-nigh breaking.
We can but pray that the coming day
Will reap, of our red sowing,
The harvest meet of a world complete
With the peace of God's bestowing.
So, with quiet heart, we do our part
In the travail of this mystery,
We give of our best, and we leave the rest
To Him Who maketh history.

Some Hymns of Thanksgiving,
Praise, and Petition for use at The
Coming Peace which, please God,
cannot now be long delayed.

TE DEUM

We thank Thee, O our God, for this
Long fought-for, hoped-for, prayed-for peace;
Thou dost cast down, and Thou upraise,
Thy hand doth order all our ways.

Lift all our hearts to nobler life,
For ever freed from fear of strife;
Let all men everywhere in Thee
Possess their souls in liberty.

Safe in Thy Love we leave our dead;
Heal all the wounds that war has made.
And help us to uproot each wrong,
Which still among us waxeth strong.

Break all the bars that hold apart
All men of nobler mind and heart;
Let all men find alone in Thee
Their one and only sovereignty!

TUNE - Old Hundredth.

THROUGH ME ONLY

Out of all the reek and turmoil
Of the dreadful battle-plain,
Came a voice insistent, calling,
Calling, calling, but in vain;
"Through Me only
Shall the world have peace again."

But our hearts were too sore-burdened,
Fighting foes and fighting pain,
And we heeded not the clear voice,
Calling, calling all in vain;
"Through Me only
Shall the world have peace again."

Now, at last, the warfare ended,
Dead the passion, loosed the strain,

Louder still that voice is calling;
Shall it call and call in vain?
"Through Me only
Shall the world have peace again."

Now we hear it; now we hearken,
In the silence of our slain,
Broken hearts new homes would build them
Of the fragments that remain.
"Through Me only
Shall the world have peace again."

Lord, we know it by our sorrows,
Might of man can ne'er attain
That Thou givest. Now we offer
Thee the Kingship. Come and reign!
Through Thee only
Shall our loss be turned to gain.

Show us, Lord, all Thou would'st have us
Do to garner all Thy grain.
Thy deep ploughing, Thy sure sowing
Richest harvest shall obtain.
Only come Thou,
Come and dwell with us again!

TUNE - Abbeycombe.

PRINCE OF PEACE

O Thou who standest both for God and Man,
O King of Kings, who wore no earthly crown,
O Prince of Peace, unto Thy feet we come,
And lay our burden down.

The weight had grown beyond our strength to bear,
Thy Love alone the woful thrall can break,
Thy Love, reborn into this world of care,
Alone can life remake.

How shall we turn to good this weight of ill?
How of our sorrows build anew to Thee?
"Of your own selves ye cannot stand or build,
Only through Me, through Me!"

O, turn once more to Thee the hearts of men,
Work through the leaven of our grief and pain,
Let not these agonies be all in vain,
Come, dwell with us again!

The world has nailed itself unto its cross;

O, tender to Thy hands its heart will prove,
For Thou alone canst heal its dreadful loss,
Come Thou and reign in love!

Peace and the sword, Lord, Thou didst come to bring;
Too long the sword has drunk to Thy decrease.
Come now, by this high way of suffering,
And reign, O Prince of Peace!

TUNE - Artavia.

"And didst Thou love the race that loved not Thee?"

THE WINNOWING

Lord, Thou hast stricken us, smitten us sore,
Winnowed us fine on the dread threshing-floor.
"Had I not reason? far you had strayed,
Vain was My calling, you would not be stayed."

Low in the dust, Lord, our hearts now are bowed,
Roughly Thy share through our boasting has ploughed.
"So as My ploughing prepares for the seed,
So shall the harvest our best hopes exceed."

Lord, we have lost of our dearest and best,
Flung to the void and cast out to the waste.
"Nay then, not one of them fell from My hand,
Here at My side in their glory they stand."

How shall we start, Lord, to build life again,
Fairer and sweeter, and freed from its pain?
"Build ye in Me and your building shall be
Builded for Time and Eternity."

TUNE - Theodora.

"Rest of the weary, joy of the sad."

TO THIS END

And hast Thou help for such as me,
Sin-weary, stained, forlorn?
"Yea then, if not for such as thee
To what end was I born?"

But I have strayed so far away,
So oft forgotten Thee.
"No smallest thing that thou hast done
But was all known to Me."

And I have followed other gods,
And brought Thy name to scorn.
"It was to win thee back from them
I wore the crown of thorn."

And, spite of all, Thou canst forgive,
And still attend my cry?
"Dear heart, for this end I did live,
To this end did I die."

And if I fall away again,
And bring Thy Love to shame?
"I'll find thee out where'er thou art,
And still thy love will claim."

All this for me, whose constant lack
Doth cause Thee constant pain?
"For this I lived, for this I died,
For this I live again."

ALL'S WELL!

Is the pathway dark and dreary?
God's in His heaven!
Are you broken, heart-sick, weary?
God's in His heaven!
Dreariest roads shall have an ending,
Broken hearts are for God's mending.
All's well! All's well!
All's ... well!

Is the burden past your bearing?
God's in His heaven!
Hopeless? Friendless? No one caring?
God's in His heaven!
Burdens shared are light to carry,
Love shall come though long He tarry.
All's well! All's well!
All's ... well!

Is the light fur ever failing?
God's in His heaven!
Is the faint heart ever quailing?
God's in His heaven!
God's strong arms are all around you,
In the dark He sought and found you.
All's well! All's well!
All's ... well!

Is the future black with sorrow?
God's in His heaven!

Do you dread each dark to-morrow?
God's in His heaven!
Nought can come without His knowing,
Come what may 'tis His bestowing.
All's well! All's well!
All's ... well!

JOHN OXENHAM – A CONCISE BIBLIOGRAPHY

God's Prisoner (1898)
Under the Iron Flail (1902)
Barbe of Grand Bayou (1903)
Bondman Free (1903)
Hearts in Exile (1904)
John of Gerisau (1904)
A Weaver of Webs (1904)
White Fire (1905)
Giant Circumstance (1906)
Profit and Loss (1906)
The Long Road (1907)
Carette of Sark (1907)
In Christ There Is No East or West (1908)
Pearl of Pearl Island (1908)
The Song of Hyacinth (1908)
My Lady of Shadows (1909)
Great Heart Gillian (1909)
A Maid of the Silver Sea (1910)
The Coil of Carne (1911)
The Quest of the Golden Rose (1912)
The Gate of the Desert (1912)
Bees in Amber (1913)
Broken Shackles (1914)
The King's High-Way (1916)
All's Well (1916)
The Fiery Cross (1917)
The Vision Splendid (1917)
High Altars (1918)
Hearts Courageous (1919)
The Wonder of Lourdes (1924)
Gentlemen - the King! (1928)
God's Candle (1929)
Hearts in Exile (1930)
The Splendour of the Dawn (1930)
The Man Who Would Save the World (1930)
The Pageant of the King's Children (1930) (with son Roderick Dunkerley)
Cross-Roads: The Story of Four Meetings (1931)
A Saint in the Making (1931)
Christ and the Third Wise Man (1934)

www.ingramcontent.com/pod-product-compliance
Lightning Source LLC
Chambersburg PA
CBHW071350130626
46556CB00005B/2110